CLOUDS CANNOT COVER US

POEMS BY JAY HULME

troika

ABOUT
CLOUDS CANNOT COVER US

We are incredibly proud at Troika to be publishing this new collection by Jay Hulme, a poet we admire profoundly and a person we have loved working with.

We think he has a unique voice and form of expression. We believe that the utter sincerity of his writing, and his voice, is strikingly powerful and deeply thought provoking. We believe Jay's voice is one that should be heard.

Jay says:
When it was decided this collection would be for teenagers I was left with this determination, that this collection wouldn't speak down to anyone, that the world I portrayed within it would be the world we live in, that there would be no attempt to make reality "appropriate for children". People seem to forget that teenagers live in the same world as everyone else, and they face the same struggles adults face every day. Teenagers deal with racism and sexism and disability and poverty and so much more that we don't even see. The things that are traditionally seen as inappropriate for young people to see, are so often the same things they experience day to day.

I remember growing up as a confused working class, transgender, young carer, and never seeing anything in literature that acknowledged any of those things. I accept that in recent years literature has become braver, with books acknowledging those things being published, but the world has also got undeniably scarier and more divisive in those years too. Despite the growth of bigotry and hatred, despite all the economic and cultural uncertainty, there's still this pervasive idea that young people should be relentlessly happy, that these years should be their best; but that's not how it works.

Some of the poems are based on, or re-worked versions of, poems I wrote when I was still in high school. Poems about the fear, and anger, and burning sense of injustice that I felt, when I looked out at the world as a teenager, and saw not only this encroaching cloud of darkness, but a constant unwillingness among those who could do something about that darkness to listen to young people like me. I think it's true that nobody listens to young people, not really. When they claim to do so, it's almost always tokenistic and patronising, but age has nothing to do with the worth of people's opinions and words. Just because someone is young, that doesn't negate their anger, or their fear, or the views they hold, and it is important to remember, and accept, that some of the views expressed in these poems, were originally formed when I was between the ages of fourteen and sixteen.

My aim, with this book, was to create something that acknowledges the dark, and the fear, and the cruelty that is all around us, but to address the fact that all is not lost, that young people are the future, not just as a clichéd saying, but as an undeniable truth. I wanted to share the truth I found in my own experience, that there is still good to be found in the world, so long as you're willing to look for it. The layout of the collection is a journey, from confusion, and fear, and anger, to hope. The poems continue, as I have done, on a journey, from the terror of a future empty of hope, to a life that is absolutely full of it. Hope can only come from within, and to create it, you first have to accept the negatives. There cannot be hope, in a perfect world, because, in a perfect world, there would be no need for it. I have been damaged by this world. In my 22 years on this Earth I have seen people die before my eyes. I have seen people I love turn from me, simply because I'm transgender. I have run from who I am, and who the world wanted me to be. I have been the victim of hate crimes, and bureaucratic incompetence. But I have seen the world try to change, and I have cultivated, in myself, a rich vein of hope, and honestly, if I could live my life again, and live it without any of the fear, or pain, or horror I have felt, then I don't think I would, because without that, I would be without hope. This book is about hope. Yes, there's darkness, but darkness only exists in contrast to light. Without one, the other cannot exist.

ONE

TWO

ONE

BIRTH

I was born with two hands
spread against white bed sheets.
My father showed this to me,
he was into photography
back then.

I was told that his eyes
were the first ones I looked to,
his misty grey meeting pale blue,
my eyes have changed like babies do,
but his have stayed the same.

Years later I found the photos,
sitting alone in a drawer of dust,
the negatives missing, the camera just
a pile of glass, a square of rust,
these memories in time.

I COME FROM

I come from two types of coffee,
cooling in the kitchen on a Monday night.
I come from eating together,
from *"Lay the table"* and *"you better eat it
because you'll get nothing else."*
I come from travel
in the back of a van,
from *"Lie down quick
so the police don't see you."*
Sleeping on a shelf,
suspended between the side panels
in the summer.

I come from garages,
and *"Pass me a spanner
from the set in the back."*
I come from oil,
dredged from the mouth
of a weeping engine.
I come from *"You can't"*
so I swear that I will.

I come from fish and chips,
and standing at the counter
as you buy wine and cigarettes at 10 p.m.
I come from fields and factories,
my dreams slipping
through cracks in the concrete,
finding their way back
on the leaves of a dandelion.

I come from school,
twelve flights of stairs
to be pushed down.
I come from bleeding knuckles,
and broken bones.
I come from concrete, and granite,
and shoes that don't fit.
I come from hope,
and find myself lost
in a world entirely bereft of it.

FOUNDATIONS

This house is built on a thousand whispers,
compacted into the earth until they became
    almost solid.
We trod them in with our boots and our words,
each syllable heavier than we ever were.
Sometimes I think we worry,
if we all stand in the same room
will the floor subside?
Are these whispers strong enough to hold us, together?
Is this house strong enough to hold us, together?
Are we strong enough to hold us together?

I wonder if whispers have ever been certified as safe,
if, as a building material, they will ever catch on.
I wonder how many houses stand on
    foundations like ours,
how many extensions were built,
    just to spread out the weight,
I wonder how many collapsed,
how many subsided.
 I wonder, how many whispers,
    when trodden into the earth,
does it take to hold up a home?

RED SEA

This house, with its carpets of sewing needles
    and thumb tacks,
spread out, glinting, like the crests of waves on the ocean.
I wonder if, when I call, my Moses will come to save me;
if he will part the tides, and show me the way.
Until that day, I am on tiptoes in my own home,
a broken ballet with too many steps en pointe,
and I, exhausted, talentless, without the training to spin,
sink, stuck, and bleeding, into this, my newly Red Sea.

832 SQUARE MILES

They said I didn't come from here,
that "here" was just a place,
    and people come from people,
but so far back as I can see,
    my family come from here.
I may have been the one to escape,
    the one to run from here, but I come from here.
My family is not the type to keep records
or to speak about the past
but I know a thing or two about our history.

I know my Grandfather's Grandfather
    worked in the mines,
all closed now for decades,
    his for generations,
his hands clawing at the spark of the seam,
in the dark of the Earth, the coal gleam,
I see his eyes like stars,
    glistening in the breathless black.

I know his Son had a motorbike
and rode it for England, drawing endless ovals
    in the clouds of dust,
and I know he did what he thought he must
when he stopped for the sake of his family,

and I know nothing of most of the others,
except that this land birthed
    their Fathers and Mothers
as it birthed mine,
and theirs,
and theirs,
and back.

And I don't care for this city,
it may be my home town,
    but I know for a fact it's not home,
but it's the place where my blood mingles
    with the earth and ploughs up a history,
where my blood mingles
    with the earth and uncovers a legacy,
smudged by the thumbprints of time.

MOTHER'S HANDS

My Mother's hands do not work anymore,
they tremble at the edges,
like magazine pages in a tornado,
like spider webs in a storm.
She used to touch type
so much faster than me,
she offered to teach
but I never took her up on it,
and now she types with one finger,
if she's lucky it makes up a word.
I heard her crying once,
when the scissors didn't work,
when the can opener didn't work,
when her hands didn't work
despite the bones she put in.
They belong to her,
thin, so thin,
stretched out like storm clouds,
trembling at the edges.

PENSION SCHEME

My Father
has been working for so long
his hands do not know
what idleness looks like.
They are always curved,
around a screwdriver, a spanner,
around the handle of a motorbike.
Somehow, they do not look like hands,
but I cannot tell you what else they could be.

And they are darker than the rest of his skin,
tanned from years on scaffolding,
and darker still where tired pores
gave up and let the oil in, that oil,
always there, for as long as I remember,
my Father coming in,
hands mottled black with that oil,
mine black with smears of ink.
I saw a symmetry there,
only his hands were broad,
vast and muscular,
the veins like vines
standing out so far
above the surface of that scaled skin.
I've never seen hands like that
on anyone else,
mystical, somehow.
Worn by so much weather.
So much work.

My Father,
his dark brown beard of my childhood,
the moustache streaked with nicotine orange,
becoming flecked with grey,
then filled with grey,
then simply grey,
with streaks of orange.
His face becoming grooved with lines,
like the isobars on a weather map.
He is not young anymore,
but he's still working.
An emergency surgery,
one organ down,
he's still working.
He will always be working.

My Father
says he must die soon,
and though his Father
almost reached his eighties
before asbestos carried him off,
my Father says sixty years old
seems like a luxury.
That he will never be a retiree.
That for a working man
the days are too empty,
and anyway,
he really doesn't have the money.
Because after years of working, over forty,
his pension pays out £2.60, annually.

So he says he will keep on working,
until one day he'll just
fall from the scaffolding,
like a bird leaving its nest
for the last time.
Fingers spread like feathers,
all the way down.

WORKING CLASS

I was born in a place where stars lose their sky,
where they fall into streetlights, to dim and die.
I was born in a place where concrete cracks
     under broken dreams,
losing the seams that hold hope together.
"Whatever the weather", we used to say,
thinking that *this* could be wished away,
like so much confetti, after a wedding.
But we were wrong.

The Ofsted reports of schools round here
say there's a culture of underachieving,
and that's kind of true.
But it's a lack of dreaming
     that's our true affliction,
a predilection for a life that's easy
destroys the dreams of the kids that, maybe,
could have done so much better.

But when your Mum and Dad,
and their Mum and Dad,
and their Mum and Dad,
have never gone to uni,
never dreamed above their station,
then it's hard to see what right
    you have to betterment.

We are the working class;
and it's true that it's hard to get out,
    but you see, I'm trying,
and even if I become some high flying millionaire
I'll never forget these streets,
where the first sheets of my story
were written.

For I, like so many others, was told not to try,
that my dreams were too high,
and there was a ceiling over the sky
to stop me from trying to reach them.
It doesn't matter though,
because dreams are what I'm made of,
and I'll make it in the end.
I have to.

A COMPREHENSIVE EDUCATION

You think that comprehensive schools fail
because the students learn less,
that we were born to earn less,
and our intelligence is somehow measurable by postcode.
But ten miles up the road
the private school makes A* students like photocopies;
every one of them born to be exceptional.
But the thing is, so are we,
but I know I'll never become Prime Minister
because my education was free,
and I never wore the old school tie
that is the fast pass to the top.

See, I can have an IQ as high as you,
but I won't get the grades,
because mine are earned in hardship;
in classrooms with leaky roofs,
and teachers who didn't pass with A's themselves.
See, I've never been taught in a school
rated higher than "satisfactory" by Ofsted,
and still some think the difference between us
is aptitude, but it isn't, it's attitude.
Cuz people round here really don't give a crap,
that's that.

We have a culture of underachievers,
and no-one believes us when we tell them our dreams,
as if we are not entitled to have them,
as if we were born for the council estate,
and people will tell us that is where we belong.
They are wrong.
Because we could be amazing,
if only some would let us.
But they won't, they don't,
and they twist the system, making it so much worse,
our prospects are travelling by hearse,
to the pit in the centre of parliament
where they bury the dreams of the poor.

DID YOU FIGHT TO BE HERE?

Did you fight to be here,
punch new things through old walls?
Did you burn the memory out,
to not face what you have done?
Did you rewrite your history with Tipp-Ex and apologies?
Did you hunt?

Did you slip down a stairwell,
when everyone was sleeping?
Each quiet footstep a prayer to the dark.
How were the shadows?
Did they dance to your touch or slide still?

Did you open books of empty phrases?
Each syllable a new fruit
unknown, and untested, and maybe unsafe.
Did you throw them across rooms, sometimes?
Break the spines?
Smooth them down with a sorry,
and a crack in your voice?

Did you fight to be here?
Were your battles the street or the page?
Were they everywhere?
Did they spiral into wars?
Fought with yourself and the world,
each on either side of a torn dust jacket
pointing rusted bayonets at the other,
as if this was worth dying for.

Maybe this is worth dying for.

THE FEET OF GIANTS

When I was little we went to Italy,
my parents took me to every gallery
that didn't have an entry fee,
and between you and me,
this will be their legacy,
because it affected me
far more than a day at Disney ever could.
The marble and wood,
creating a temple that connects
not God and Man
but us with our souls,
filling the holes in our hearts
with paint and glue,
whispering in every language
that you
yes, *you*,
were the only person
this painting was made for.

And when we stared at the statues,
and my light up shoes
shone flashing blues
on the feet of giants,
hands reaching out
to moments beyond my imagining,
I knew that *this* is what we were made for.
Not a gallery tour,
but a moment, alone,
with Michelangelo's David,
or Botticelli's Venus,
as they speak to us;
and though the words are in some
unknown tongue,
that even the multi-lingual
guidebooks can't translate,
it's like fate, whispering in your ear.
And once you've been here, you know,
exactly which direction
your soul needs to go.

POETRY

Poetry may not be a choice form,
the norm through which
    a point may movement make,
but to all the outcasts, and play casts,
    and class acts, and classes,
to those whose hearts scream
    for more than cholesterol and blood,
it's the visceral, vital, vile truths of honesty,
    clothed in ink and paper.

To the smoke brained child with grasping hands,
dreaming of lands beyond a mind's imagining.
To the sane faced, sad eyed, psychopath in black,
whose crime was writing truths
    in the inkwell of his skull.
To the fancy boy, with broken bones,
tones lighter than summer in a wanton fog
of bliss, and burden, and endless,
    glistening rainbows.
To the hopeful heart of scorned love,
pretentious prejudice paralysing its aortas
with prose so dense, even ideas cannot pass.
To the girl who dreams of apartment blocks,
on turbulent seas of music and magazine pages.
To the teacher, with hands smeared in ink,
and the tears of pupils,
    with no-one else to confide in,
the hopes of a generation,
    riding on their shoulders of stone.

To these it is truth,
    for they know in their cores:
that though many think poetry
    is the words that comprise it,
the whole that they make
    is magic surpassing
the sum of these singular parts.

THE YOUNG

We walk through alleyways
between broken streetlights,
flickering in time
with our headstrong heartbeats,
neither naïve nor brave,
but somehow apathetic
at the prospect of the danger
we are in.

Our pockets are empty
except for our hands,
and our minds are drowning
in far off lands,
and our ears are ringing
from echoing bands,
and somehow we never go home.

We keep on stepping
but we never leave,
and our lungs are heaving
the smog we breathe,
and we keep on yelling,
we boil and seethe,
and somehow we never atone.

Our throats just scream
at conformity,
as we listen to bands
we're too skint to see,
and all that we want
is just to be free,
and somehow we're always
alone.

FLYING'S LIKE FALLING

I don't know much about anything,
but I'm good with words
cuz words are like flying,
and flying's like falling,
and I'm good at falling.

I've kissed the ground so many times,
I scratched rhymes into the earth, with my fingernails,
hoping one day my fails will become passes,
and I will fly for the first time.

When I was a kid, I dreamed I had wings like an angel,
I found my halo in a box in the pub car park,
it was a stark reality that hit me when I realised dreams
don't come true – especially not the happy ones.

But I keep on writing,
because sometimes I get a man-made halo
when the lights are low on stage,
    and my hair reflects it a bit,
and from where you sit,
    I could have wings under my shirt.
Because maybe dreams don't come true,
but it doesn't hurt to have them,
after all when I fall the only reason I get back up
is the thought that one day, I will fly.

Because words, they're just like flying,
and flying's like falling.
And one day I'm gonna find
I have wings on the way down,
and a halo as a crown,
and one day –
I, am gonna fly.

FINDING MY VOICE

When I was younger I got into so many fights
I can't remember which back street
    I left my teeth in,
I'm amazed I'm breathing;

Because I really should have lost more fights,
it didn't put the world to rights, but it felt better –
and maybe that was just some post fist-fight
    adrenaline rush,
but it was enough to push me down,
    and let me relax.

Looking back, it's scary,
that the only thing between me, and expulsion,
were my high grades, and an ability to admit,
that what I was doing, was wrong.

But I was headed for a swan song,
a morning where my anger wasn't enough to let me win
because living life by the skin of your teeth isn't easy,
and if you don't get out young, you're stuck there.

So I ran – so far and so fast
    I shed the skin of my past
and found a new soul – one that's whole,
not bruised by too many hits. And yeah,
    bits of me are different,
but I can ignore an affront, and get down
    my anger in words.

Cuz I found a voice – my voice,
a way to show the heart of me non violently,
and honestly, I'm certain it's saved my life.

THE JUDGE

You hold court in your Reebok trainers,
claiming lies and lives,
sending down sentences
like repossession orders,
their names handed over like currency
leaving them bereft
of self.

Branding some with the title "snitch",
a white hot burn
on their fading reputation,
no alleviation will come
when their name is synonymous with outcast,
and your sentence hangs over their being,
for no parole is offered
to the broken, branded man.

And the women are labelled "whores",
vilified behind closed doors
then sentenced by declaration,
for the world to see.
A prosecution based on prostitution,
a sordid mix of lies and rumour,
and the damning arm of circumstance,
for if they dare to give a man a dance,
they're doomed.

You preside over your estate,
concrete halls, and cinder block walls,
1960's temples with spires to the sky,
techno fading into courthouse whispers,
and the only proof you need
is on the side of a bottle,
as you drink to the futures
of those you condemn.
Social pariahs, strung up on the pyres
you build on the balconies
when you declare them
unclean.

WHEN CHILDREN ARE MEN

His mouth was empty from all that came before it,
the past writ large on his stretching skin,
it is hard to know where to find your kin
in this wasteland of a home.

They say the palms of your hands
tell the truths of your life,
but the lines that you find here
are written in blood.

They say a man cannot change,
they say this man cannot change,
he is a boy in his being
but his bearing betrays him;
he is a child forced into a man.

They say his eyes are like earthquakes,
they shift every second.
They take in the world
like a child in the light,
I know that he's seen me,
long before he accepts that I'm there.

They say his name is a danger,
that his legs carry murder,
that his age is unnoticed,
that his heart is broken,
that he refuses to accept this
citywide hatred,

they say this boy is a man,
and they say some men,
some boys,
can never be redeemed.

HE DROWNED THE BEE

He drowned the bee,
snatched it from me,
dropped it in whiskey,

and I saw the Earth die
in his eyes.
In that moment I realised:

Here is a man
who kills the defenceless,
to feel power as if it is his.

THE MASTERY OF MEN

All around the world
women are placing their broken teeth
under their pillows,
praying that the tooth fairy will become
their guardian angel,
to keep them safe from the fists
that rest unclenched beside them
in this too small bed.
His unspoken apology,
even without a voice
screams *lies* beneath the covers.
As if an insincere *sorry* is enough
to cover the bruises those hands left,
and the imprint of his wedding ring,
the greatest insult given across her hips.

Her clenched lips,
the frown that scars her forehead,
like the history of gasoline
on some unnamed sister
in the far flung East.
She hears the stories,
muffled through the radio,
trying to decide if self immolation
is courage or cowardice,
too scared to choose
in case she decides
it's just the easiest way out.

She wants to shout,
raise her hands to rend the sky,
until the constellations mirror
the markings of her mind,
she wants to leave this behind,
find the memory of herself
in the shipwreck she's become,
turn his twisted words into speeches,
screaming: "You need to get out. Now!"

But sometimes he smiles,
and she thinks that it's genuine,
like it was when she married him,
because he used to be lovely,
or she was just naïve.
It doesn't matter anymore.
They're bound by law.
And the wedding ring she chose
has become a manacle.
Bound in white gold and diamond,
she is a woman,
trapped in the mastery of men.

DARKNESS WALKED

The Dark walked into her
closed her eyes, and walled up spaces,
made places even she cannot touch.
Her mascara formed storm clouds,
whorls of black upon her skin
like the clouds that filled her mind,
when Darkness walked in.

Her dreams lost themselves in repetitions,
every night, every corridor,
every movement the same.
She thought that she would die of shame,
that, or drown in sin,
she turned to blame herself,
when Darkness walked in.

For what else could she do,
so silenced as she was?
A victim bound by stigma,
becoming ever lost.
She looked towards her future,
saw a place she'd never be,
and never said to anyone:

"Darkness walked in me."

RED SKIES

The sky is red tonight,
some say blood was spilled,
the city holds its breath,
everything is still.

I KNEW A MAN

I knew a man who killed a man,
who shot a man;
who knew a man.
I knew a man who shot a man,
who killed a man
he knew.

And I knew a man who died alone,
was shot alone;
who died unknown.
I knew a man who died alone,
before the man
he knew.

And I knew a woman who stayed at home,
who cried at home;
who cried alone.
I knew a woman whose broken home,
was haunted
by the two.

A WORLD WITHOUT GUNS

There isn't an answer,
so I'm not asking why
you carry bullets,
when no-one must die,
and they're packaged in sixes,
and shot to the sky,
and the truth is one bullet
is a lifetime supply.

And people bring guns
to the church or the store,
and this need for weapons
is their deadliest flaw,
because if you use your brain,
then you need nothing more,
than your words and your reason,
not murder by law.

And if you didn't have guns
in your shops and your bars,
then you wouldn't need guns
in your pockets and cars,
and if it's true that the dead,
become glimmering stars,
then in a world without guns,
half the sky would be ours.

HOW THINGS ARE FIXED

They paint over the graffiti,
blocks of colour slapped in off shades
across green fences and black gates,
and they say this is healing:
that this is how things are fixed.

I remember the colours:
the outdoor gallery,
the only place to see, for free,
the physical result of dreams,

but they said it was vandalism.
That making a mark in this city
is a criminal action.
That painting your heart in this city
is worse than what they've done,

those boxes,
the same size and shape as all that's gone before;
censored frames plastered on brick walls.
One day they'll paint the whole city
some off shade of black,
and I know, in my heart, that the people who do
won't see what's wrong with that.

I SEE YOU

It seems like every few minutes,
in every town centre,
I search every pocket of my coat,
to find something worth giving away.
A gift to say: I see you,
I see you, and I am sorry.

I wish I could say:
here is a handwritten apology
for the state of society;
here is a hotel key card,
and a warm bed;
here is a fragment of my heart
to keep warmth inside you;
here is a winning lottery ticket,
and the ability to know it has won;
here is a coat worthy of Everest
for every other street corner.
Here is a flat.
Here is a house.
Here is a home.

I have none of these things in my pockets,
my hands itch with their own cold.
I see the weeks I spent hanging
between rented rooms,
and those same prolific pavements.
I see the safety nets I scraped together
at the very last second,
I see the luck,
I see you,
and I am sorry.

CONSUMED

Cities eat people, he said;
these windows are not eyes,
but mouths,
and we are consumed.

Mostly, cities eat souls, he said;
they spit the bodies out,
I see them every day,
in the streets.

WAR FINDS WAYS

We name our streets after battles,
and wonder why violence visits them.
But we cannot question pointless death
when we place war so highly,
we find our way with it.

THE BEAUTY OF UTTER DESTRUCTION

Have you ever seen the souls?
Shining so brightly
through the cracks in the faces,
of the survivors waiting,
for those who will never return.

Have you ever seen the sky burn?
In the moments before the bombs fall,
and the fates of those below are set.

Have you ever seen the slow pirouette?
Of a man caught by artillery fire,
trapped between defiance and realisation,
in the instant before he falls.

Have you ever seen the calls?
For men of a nation to take up arms,
pasted on walls like postage stamps,
sending the youth of a country to die
on foreign soil.

Have you ever seen the oil?
Spilling from the wreck of a downed plane,
a rainbow shimmering in the fire's heat,
as the pilot, trapped in the midst
of his own Viking funeral,
lays his hand upon a portrait
of his Mother.

Have you ever seen the brother?
Standing beside the grave of his twin,
shoulders drowned by the weight
of his duty.

Have you ever seen the beauty?
That hides in the moments of pause,
that give clarity in the midst of wars
and their utter destruction.

THEY ARE MEN

They are men,
conquering the skies with joystick scythes,
in every inch that's conquered, eyes,
from above stare down
on the fire.

They are men,
fighting battles on monitor screens
scratching off targets and inbetweens,
who knows what it means
from a distance.

They are men,
capturing cities they've never been to,
from men they've never met,
their silhouette still stained
on a canvas wall.

They are men,
though they act barely human at all.

SADNESS IS A SONG

Sadness is a song
you hear when the birds
falter at first light,
when the night is
newly broken,
but not yet forgotten.
Not past enough
to make it seem safe.

Sadness is a song
you hear between heartbeats,
when the blood flow
falls silent,
and you hear
the nothing of death
inhabit the living.

Sadness is a song
stitched into the sunshine,
that line of
not quite here,
that makes the day
break character.

Sadness is a song
slipping from the throats
of every person
forced to scream
their loved one's name
in mourning.

Sadness is a song
that hides in the cracks
of the silences
we desperately want
to disprove.

THE LOST

His fist forms the skyline of a bombed out city,
you see its dying embers in his eyes.
When he holds out his hand
you see bodies falling,
crumpling backwards,
one at a time.

His shoulders form hills
like the sand dunes he walked through,
shifting together, in separate lines.
When he hunches right over
you can almost see them,
the lost struggling onwards,
they cling to his spine.

His mouth forms the pits where his brothers are buried,
they live in his dreams from different times,
he carried them with him,
'cross so many oceans.
He prays for his family,
his homeland,
his life.

HAMSAS

They've spray painted hamsas on the underpasses,
they say it wards off evil eyes,
    and I know which in particular.
They hope when the immigration officials,
guardians of this new hostile environment,
    where nothing is allowed to grow,
come and look for them,
    their evil eyes will slip at the symbols.
That the tangled roots of a dozen countries
    will stay planted,
that they cannot erase this garden
    from the landscape,
that every gnarled branch and new growth,
every flower and fruit and thorn
    stay tied to this new earth.
For every gardener knows transplantations
    are dangerous,
and some in this circle of hands
    have never known new soil.

GODS BEHIND GLASS

There was a Monk at the museum,
burning like sunset in the gloom
as he stares at his God behind glass,

this stolen God
holds memories of massacres
of which we will never speak.

The plaque below states date of discovery,
as if white men hold a monopoly
on the moment things start to exist.

NINETY DEGREES

When they placed set squares
on their Mercator projections,
they didn't see the people; in their

need to make the world
a chessboard, neatly dividing
forever, the black from white.

They just drew their lines,
straighter than anything
nature provides.

The concept of people as
property not forgotten
in this time, and objects need

only a carefully made
box to stay in. Ninety
degrees at all the edges.

PITTSBURGH, OCTOBER 27TH, 2018
For Natalie H.

She goes to the vigil,
not because she is without fear,
but because she is scared.
She wonders if she is next.

In Europe the synagogues are locked.
She wonders if hers will do the same,
employ guards outside that holy place
to keep the fear out.

She wishes there were guards inside her,
so they could do the same.
That night she sees her ancestors,
lost in mass graves.

They wanted to erase her, she sees,
take people like her off city streets,
she says tomorrow she will live as normal,
despite mists of defiance and fear.

She says when others try to erase you,
it's heroic to show you are here.

*On the 27th of October, 2018, a white supremacist killed eleven
innocent worshippers in the Tree of Life Synagogue in Pittsburgh,
Pennsylvania, USA.*

CHRISTCHURCH, MARCH 15TH, 2019

When hatred comes it comes in pieces.
It sits in the silences in between words,
when it seems too small to correct,
when it seems too big to correct,
when no one cares anymore,
when it's justified.
When it's revenge for the past,
the future,
the imagined.

Hatred comes when nobody's looking,
and stays until everyone is.
It's in the stories we don't tell,
in the words we don't say,
in the people we don't speak to,
or care for,
or love.
It comes in us,
it comes as us.

When hatred comes, it comes in pieces,
and leaves pieces in its wake.

On the 15th of March, 2019, a white supremacist killed fifty innocent worshippers at the Al Noor Mosque and Linwood Islamic Centre in Christchurch, New Zealand.

COBWEBS AND FOXGLOVES

War smiles,
his teeth are assault rifles,
he turns his horse's head to the West
and shoulders his sword.
Man has made weapons of war
more powerful than he.

Famine crouches in the dust,
his paper skin smudges at the edges
as he buries himself in the earth.
There is no comfort here.
The flies search the riverbed for rot
and find nothing.

Pestilence touches the child,
who touches the child,
who touches the child,
who holds his Grandmother's hands.
He has seen the world reborn,
and believes in sharing.

Death holds hands with his brother
and jumps with him from the edge,
unknowing now if he leads or follows.
He spreads his arms to encompass the Earth
and his hands are strung with cobwebs
and foxgloves.

THE DELAY OF THE NUMBER 73 BUS
(due to pedestrian collision)

Who knew that death could come so quick?
Who felt their life so fleeting?
Who knew that flesh could be so weak,
Who heard the darkness seeking?
Who stood their ground within the crowd,
Who watched this fate deliver?
Who felt the halting breath rebound?
Who saw this young life wither?

Who saw the future fade away?
Who saw the minutes die?
Who held your hand, and learned your name,
Who soothed you with a lie?
Who watched you fade like edge of dawn,
Who called the sirens closer?
Who watched your soul just flit away?
Who saw you to your maker?

TWO

OH FATHER

Oh Father, take these hands,
they claw at the foundations
you built us on, oh Father.
Take these cracked palms,
these bruised knuckles,
this riotous flesh, oh Father.
Take the nails that clawed
at my own coffin,
take these bony fingers,
too thin to plug the holes
in this sinking ship, oh Father.
I could not save myself
with these hands,
so take them from me.

Oh Father, swallow this name,
in the solidifying seconds
of a whirlwind breath,
take it deep into your lungs
like cigarette smoke,
and form its syllables into clouds
as you breathe it back out, oh Father.
Let it drift into the nether,
let it fall into the cracks of speech
I open up with my own heartbeat, oh Father.
Beat it back into the jungle of breaking tongues,
lose it in mistimed gestures,
and peeling words, oh Father.
This name is not my own,
so take it from me.

Oh Father, take these eyes,
they see only into the darkness
at the end of the stars, oh Father.
The truth can be warped
by an optical nerve,
and none tells more lies
than my own, oh Father.
Grasp them in your storied palms,
teach them what truth is
in the darkness you made for them, oh Father.
They say the eyes are the windows to the soul
but mine remain empty,
tell me, what does that mean?
I think these eyes are corrupted
by the weight of the world,
so take them from me.

Take all of this from me.
Take all of me from me.
Oh, Father.

DROWNING

I watched you drowning
in the waters of life,
unable to struggle.

The eerie silence
of a drowning man
clamours in my ears,

head tilted to the sky,
as a man hoping the Gods
would see his tears,

before they met the sea,
mingled with the water,
and were lost.

I hope a lifeguard spots
all he was trained to see
in your pleading eyes,

dismissing the lies
of TV drama
to understand,

that screaming and splashing
don't mark the drowning.
It is eerie silence,

and slow movements,
that are the cries for help
of the dying.

FOOLS

We were fools,
so sure of who we were
we forgot what was in our hearts,
like this, we ran, empty of ourselves,
in fields strewn with broken glass,
feet cut to ribbons,
hearts of denial,
in parting, I looked within,
and found myself,
whole and mocking.
A reminder of what I could have been.

I AM A MAN

I am a man.
A touch too short
in children's clothes,
rows of yellow teeth
open like doors into nowhere
to correct a pronoun – or twenty.
Plenty of mistakes are accidents.
Plenty are not.

I hold my head bowed
in public places,
feeling so strongly
the gaps and the spaces
where parts of my body should be,
for though the man within
belongs here,
he belongs in fear
of the actions of others.

Brothers.
I stand in fear of you –
Of the fists you hold beside you.
Of the fists you hold inside you.
Of your pistol lips,
issuing words like pistol whips,
swear words crack
and the pretence slips,
and I am always falling.
One syllable at a time.

The line is always the same:
I'm not a man
they say.
I tell a lie
they say.
I'm a freak
they say.
I should die
they say.

Words.
They never quite leave you.
My life is traced in scar tissue,
along the paths these shrapnel syllables
have scorched into my history.
The symmetry of my skin
is broken by the past within
and I cannot begin to name
the cause of every wound.

But here is birth,
and here is worth,
and here is fear,
and fault, and earth.
And here is girls' PE class,
and gendered groups,
and bras, and pants,
and shirts with scoops
for necklines.

And here are my fault lines,
rewinds, first times.
Here are long hairdos,
and women's loos,
and how to choose
a knife or noose.

And here is self hatred,
I created a hedonistic horror show
out of my own torso.
Tore my skin into cobwebs
to capture my demons,
bloodied fists in fights
about rules and regulations,
and tried to hide
the scars upon my skin.

I was born to never win,
to never sin,
to quietly sit
and never sing.
Never express myself,
never search for wealth,
never care for health.

I was born to be a blank canvas
for my parents' failed dreams,
and it seems to me that I
have failed in that duty,
and the beauty of it all
is I don't care anymore.

My fists forget my own face.
When, out of place,
I erase my morals
in a fight for morality.
The shattered skin of me
is draped on every shaking tree,
like the breaths I take,
breaking when no-one can see me.

I left my family.
In the shadow of that skin,
in the shadow of the person
that could never let them in,
in the shadow of the person
they could never see the truth within,
I left them shouting.

Pitchforks raised to chase away
the man I have become.
I left them, on a hurricane Tuesday.
When the weather broke against me
like the wrath of a God
others told me existed.

I left my family without hesitation,
without breaking my stride,
without breaking my pride,
without looking back.
Because the lack of regret on their faces
would have written my gravestone.

I walked alone
into the alleyways of life,
knife tucked into my jacket
to fight for my future,
palms pressed bloody
over scar and suture,
wishing my mind
was as easy to fix
as my skin.

Sometimes I think of a world of lies,
of family, and brevity,
of lightness, and of levity,
a world where I can stand as me
unburdened by this mask you see,
it sends me down to purgatory
and hides my shining soul.

But whenever it breaks.
Is less than whole.
I fix it.
For it hides more than me,
you see,
it hides a bullet shot
the moment I was born,
worn smooth
from years of probing,
it says,
a word
that has never been
my name.

PICTURE QUALITY

I see photos taken way back,
before I was born,
before my Father was born,
and in them I see us.
Marching with signs,
calling for equality.
Only equality.

I look into the eyes
of those marching with signs,
on streets I do not recognise,
holding a sign I've seen before
a thousand times,
and I see me in their eyes;
because what you have to realise
is the only difference between us and them,
is the difference in the picture quality.
Because we still fight for equality.

So why do we carry on marching?
With placards, and whistles, and flags,
why do we carry on calling
for our rights to be equal to yours?
Because rights are not rights if they are wrong,
and our rights are wrong.
.They are dreams of a minority
pushed aside by society,
and equality is a fantasy,
in the ears of the oppressed.
We do not stand with the rest.
And your human rights list is torn,
where are the missing pages?
Where are the missing pages?

Where are the clauses that tell us:
We are not scum.
We are not queers.
We are not trannies.
We are people.
Where are the clauses that tell us:
I can determine my gender,
and no-one can be judged
by the actions of another,
and the media fuelled fears
that block the veins of this society
like poison,
are wrong.

So we will keep on fighting,
until we are equal to you.
Because these photos,
in black and white,
blurry and crumpled,
are not a sign of failure;
they are fuel for the fire
of the anger today,
and if we cannot be change,
you can be sure,
we will fuel it.

So take photos of me,
standing with my sign in the same place,
but a different face,
and let the picture quality show
how much time has passed,
because this anger will last.
And you can laugh at us,
and tell us we have no chance,
that we will fail.
You can tell us:
shut up,
sit down,
and listen.
And we will say:
No.
You listen.

Because your ears are filled with lies,
the fears of the media,
righteous rhetoric,
pointing at things that never even happened;
but I see clearly,
that this broken up society
needs to change,
we will be change,
we will fuel change,
so take my photo,
place it under a mocking header,
jeer at me in your paper,
because all you are doing
is giving me a chance,
to be the photo that rekindles
the fire.

BROADMEAD

They told me I was Satan,
those street side preachers
with gospel grin,
whose outstretched arms
with leaflets in
never quite reach
to the edge of their sin,

their righteous piety stretched
into elastic smiles
that snap back in
at the sight of people like me.

If Jesus walked he'd apologise
to the ground beneath their feet,
that self deceit
required to turn others,
I wonder if they formed
a believer even once.

IN THE FUTURE

In the future nobody will ever be scared
to walk into a bathroom, or any room. Ever.
People'll be allowed to be their own gender,
there will be no loopholes in laws,
precedents promoting hatred
allowing panic at our existence
to excuse our murders.
In the future people like me
will not be able to distinctly describe
the scent of the floor in the men's toilet
that time they were slammed into it,
and if, in the future, they could,
they'd feel able to report it,
instead of going home, showering in the dark,
and feeling lucky.
Like the one that got away.

I could have died that day, or any day,
and as I write these words down
I'm painfully aware
that someone out there might
want to kill me for living so freely,
and honestly, I'm watching my back.
I'm always watching my back.
I've forgotten what my face looks like
but can easily describe my spine.
The way it bends under pressure,
the way it curves, but will not break.

ON LEAVING

He says that I have changed,
that I have mellowed somehow,
that the whirl of fists
always waiting to pass my lips
has, in this year, given way
to some form of compassion.

He says my bricked up heart
that I sacked and drowned,
in a river not far from where I grew up,
must have finally returned to me.

He says that my spine,
that was always curved
under the weight of the hate
I bore for the world,
is becoming a plumbline,
falling straight and true.

He says, in his opinion,
the love and happiness
he has seen in the last few days
is nothing less than a miracle.

He says, perhaps it is true
that people can change,
not quickly, or all at once,
but in the course of months,
when no-one is really looking.

He says he saw me smile more
in these three days
than he did in the last eight years.

He says he thinks this life
has come good for me,
that I am happy.

He says he'll see me soon,
and steps onto the bus,
still questioning
where this change
has come from.

I look to the South,
through the walls of this city,
and across those rolling hills,

I say I know exactly
where it has come from,
but though I can give
coordinates to a place,
I cannot give them
to a heart.

He doesn't hear me,
his shoulder pressed
to the window pane
shifts slightly,
and I turn,
slowly.
Away.

QUEEN CHARLOTTE STREET

All this light on my windows,
an expressionist painting,
I stare at the lines
but they don't mean a thing.
My hands are the same
as the past that's been tracing
the path of the rain
as it's starting to thin.

WATER OF LIFE

My friend, a nurse,
cries in quiet rooms
when no-one can hear her.
Her grief becomes a whirlwind,
a storm that threatens
to blow the roof away
and let in the sky.

But sometimes, on good days,
the young do not die,
and she brings home her tears
and shares them;
as if they could be the water of life,
as if she's trying to give us all
a piece of their power.

JUST THE SMALL THINGS

I'm going to build a factory
    where happiness is made,
where it can be laid on every surface
like a damp balloon popped in a water fight,
there will not be a cathedral of light,
no cinematic runs through airports,
just the small things.

Like the memories you know are etched in rings,
the taste of lemonade made from your lemons,
so distinctly different from any others,
the taste of your brother's name on your lips
as you welcome him home.
The foam on coffee,
the branch of the tree you fell from
    when you were six,
the sticks whipping your ankles on the way down,
and the shadow of a frown beneath
    your Father's smile,
the coolness of tile beneath bare feet,
the joy when you eat,
and the feeling of a dog,
dreaming as it sleeps on your knees.

Playing Scrabble with a child
who announces with such conviction
that she will become an astronaut,
or a dolphin,
and she believes in it so wholly
you cannot imagine it not coming true.
The smiley face graffitied on a bathroom mirror,
the steam becoming a canvas
that can only ever repeat.
The pad of feet on old carpets,
smiles when you least expect them,
the whispers of a voice declaring:
you have come home.
Home.
Home.

In this factory I will not manufacture your dreams.
And though that seems like a faux pas,
people mix up dreams and happiness,
and when they wish for your dreams to come true
they seem forget that nightmares are dreams too.
I will not form the castles you see in your sleep,
none of the flash cars or fine wines,
there will be lines on the skin of your face
as you pass through the future,
but you will be happy. You see,
happiness is not made of dreams,
it is made of the tiny things you forget
when the storm rolls in.

BEAUTY'S A CONSTRUCT

Our image of beauty
is not set in stone,
you can't carve a Madonna
that's not truly your own,
and if you judge others
then I hope you atone,
for the wrongs that you do,
in the life that you're loaned.

We cannot judge others
by just what we see,
the ideals you chase
aren't what a person should be,
and as some love the land,
and some love the sea,
the beauty I long for
is tailored to me.

So wherever you go,
and wherever you're led,
remember the truth
as you lay in your bed,
remember this poem,
and all that's been said:
beauty's a construct,
it's all in your head.

SO MANY BOYS

My sister is showering,
I sit on the lid of the toilet
as she tells me about boys.
All of the boys.
So many boys.

I hand her the face wash,
see the whisk of the curtain,
the damp closing,
her stretched silhouette
on white fabric,

tomorrow, I will drive her to the clinic,
where she will tell them
about the boys.
All of the boys.
So many boys.

I close my eyes, and hand her a towel.
When I ask if *they're* worth it
she smiles,
and says:
Boys never are.

I think, for a moment, about the boys.
All of the boys.
So many boys.
I ask if *it's* worth it
Yes. She says.

Every time.

PILLARS OF STONE

I heard you never danced in public,
but last night I saw you do the foxtrot,
alone amongst the pews
of the church just down the road
        from where I live now.
When I asked you how you live like this,
how you dance like this,
alone atop the gravestones,
you tell me your dance sounds
        like rain to the dead.
That they're dreaming of water.

I embraced you,
stiff armed like something stood between us,
as if suddenly you found the Conservatives' Jesus.
As if he existed in this gap that we made,
as if he was here, creating shame.

I climbed the bell tower,
stared out from the wooden slatting,
heard the bells ring,
so close to my bones they moved everything.
One inch to the left and out
        of my person a touch,
I wonder if that's good,
if "me" was too much.

And I held out my arms again,
not stiff, and more knowing than before,
I saw the war in your soul and I held it.
Withstood the bullets you fired into yourself,
that ricocheted through
    the pillars of stone
of this church I found myself in,
bouncing from fears made of churning bone,
I saw they made you.
I saw they knew you.
Like I did.

So we climbed the belfry
like bats at dawn,
holding hands in a spiral staircase
    barely wide enough for one,
and the bells rang our song:
one inch to the left and out of our bodies a touch –
and I heard the rain falling,
    not too loud, or too much
and in this wedding dance from the dead
we dreamed of water.

FORESTS OF MEMORY

I am sorry for the forests of memory.
The forests that grew in your lungs,
the forests you tried to clear
with the smoke of cigarette after cigarette.
The forests that linger yet.

I am sorry for the evergreen sorrow,
roots broad as branches,
choking tomorrow, I am sorry
for the seeds that I held.
For the seeds that were sown.

I am sorry for the roughness of bark,
pressing so tightly
against your echoing lungs,
the lungs that are filling with wind song.
I cannot right this wrong.

And I am sorry.
I'm sorry your smoke can't start fire,
I'm sorry that I am a liar,
I'm sorry for the love of the branches
that are taking over your core.

I'm sorry that I'm not brave enough,
not proud enough,
not kind enough,
I'm sorry that I can't love enough,
to prune the forests I leave.

UNFINISHED PORTRAIT

You were the drawing I never finished,
not because you were ugly but
because I was too scared of finishing.

I would return once a fortnight
to make little changes and rub out
the tiny hairy lines of pencil that
swirled around your face.

But I was too scared
of the inks and the watercolours,
I was too scared of the finality
of the mistakes I could make.

For if I scarred you it would be forever,
and if I started again it wouldn't be you,
so I wasted the years,
staring at an unfinished portrait,
and imagining the beauty within.

I SAY

I am not the Earth,
I say to the sky.
I cannot hold the weight
of these people upon my skin,
I cannot hold the weight
of this past upon my skin,
I am not the Earth.

I say this fire inside me
is far fiercer than a volcano,
and there are no such things
as controlled implosions.
I say if I were a star,
I would fold into myself,
I say this fire.

The sky does not listen,
so I pluck a star
from the branches
of oblivion's arms,
and whisper these truths
into its light, but the sky,
the sky does not listen.

THE MEANING OF STORIES

Perhaps it is true that none of my heroes exist,
summed up on a list entitled "fictional characters".
My life lessons come from the mouths
of people paid to pretend they are
        someone they're not,
but I can't forget what they have taught me.

Because when words mean something,
        they stay,
no matter where they came from.
So who cares if I live my life by a line
issued from the mouth of Gandalf the Grey,
        on a film set,
it doesn't mean it's worth less than something
said by someone who actually existed.
Because attribution is overshadowed by meaning,
and the fact that these words stay with me
means more than the circumstances
under which they were uttered.

So if fiction is the foundation
on which I build my life, I can promise you
that my turrets will reach the sky,
before yours reach my dungeons.
Because fiction holds within it
the promise of a better world;
and I believe,
not just because I can,
but because I have to.

THE LETTERS WE LOSE

You scratched a line
through the Sharpie scrawl
on your overpriced latte,
saying something about how "today…"
"Today was amazing!"
But I was gazing,
somewhat distractedly,
at the remnant of Sharpie
caught under your fingernail.
A fine black veil
made up of part of your name,
and though you can't read it
it's your name just the same,
and I really have to wonder:
What happens to the letters we lose?

What happens to the vowel sounds
we leave scattered in the chalk dust?
The words in books everyone fussed about,
so much that they were left burning?
The pencilled words that even now
are turning into rubber shavings?
The dry wipe pen marks
from every whiteboard in the world?
What happens to the letters we lose?

I like to imagine they are caught,
on our shoes, on our skin, in our cavernous lungs.
I like to imagine they bleed into us, one syllable at a time.
I like to imagine that the burnt books of Alexandria
are floating in the air somewhere,
waiting for someone to breathe them in.
I like to imagine that every cleared piece of illegal graffiti
is lingering in the water table,
until it is able to be swallowed,
and spat back out again.
I like to imagine that language is a game,
with only so many tiles,
and they travel for miles,
unnoticed on the soles of your shoes.

You look up at me,
lost in my far away daydream,
and I seem like I don't care,
and I kind of don't,
but in a bit I will,
honestly.

I was just too busy catching the letters,
you caught, and stored, and threw at me.

GUIDE YOU HOME

Ghostly ships pass in the night,
their sails stripped of silver light
for orange.
Glowing out across the water,
colliding with the past,
colliding into nothing,
the walk is quiet.
The city never sleeps, but it is still.
Those who pass move like fragments
of broken VHS tapes;
the video moves on without them.

The stars are gone from here
but we made our own,
collected from the hills
and forced into fairy lights.
Strung on homes,
and ships,
and the fragments of bridges.
If you're lost, pick spires from the mist,
they will guide you home.

Take back this city,
this history,
divide it equally,
share it with everybody.
Build shrines across Redcliffe
where our ancestors are buried,
visit them daily,
or on weekends.
Place the past inside the future,
keep it safe from our hands,
blend it seamlessly;
like walking down Park Street
to the Harbour.

Send ships out to sea
without reason to go.
Wave from the bridges,
from the woods,
from Clifton.
Remember who we were,
who we are,
where those things meet.
Stand on the pavement,
stare out at the roads,
at the shrapnel pecked history,
at the ruins;
at the past we kept as a reminder,
at the future we're building every second,
at the now,
at the edges,
at the inbetween.

Reach out your hands,
let them skim by the skyline,
caress the cranes,
and the bridges,
and the spires you see;
settle on rooftops,
and call to the birds.
Hold home condensed
in the palm of your hand
as the sun casts shadows of every fingertip.
Hold the breath of this place
in the seconds it takes you
to time your life in this sundial;
calibrate the spires,
line them up with your dreams,
then breathe.

Shake hands with your shadow
as it crosses Queen's Square,
know this city is home,
that it's always been there.

IN A THOUSAND YEARS

What will they say of us
in a thousand years?
When the planet is dead or dying,
when they come
to watch over us,
dig over us,

when our graves are not graves
but archaeological sites;
when our prayers are not prayers
but indigenous rites;
when our roadways are artworks,
when our buildings are ruins,

when our writings are gone
or untranslatable,
when our art is faded
or forgotten entirely,
when the poets come
behind the historians,

what will they say of us?
In languages we never imagined,
I would hope it is truth,
or some semblance of it.
But history is simply fantasy
written with fragments of fact.

DISTANCE

I've spent so many sleepless nights
staring out of silent windows,
wishing for the stars.
Reaching hands into the void
as if I could hold them,
never once realising they seem so close
only because they're so far away,
and in the day,
I dream of starships and astronauts,
men in far off galaxies,
staring at different stars,
and even the ones that are ours,
but from a different angle.
And I imagine aliens
incorporating our sun
into their own constellations,
drawing lines in the sky
with their fingers
as they tell tales of distant lands,
their hands stretched out as far as mine
in some parody of mime
played out on different edges
of the universe.
And I don't know what's worse,
the idea that they have no concept of me,
or that they reflect, like I,
on the boundless distance between us.

EXISTENTIALISM

When you think about it,
nothing we do matters.
We are atoms, lost on a planet,
drowning in the blackness
and the vastness of space.
We are nothing.
Our hopes and dreams
mean the same as the ambitions
of the ants being crushed
on the busy A6
and when we die,
as we will,
we are forgotten to history,
for no matter what we do,
we are ghosts in time.

So mess up,
because nothing you do
matters to anyone but you.
So who cares about the time
you made a fool of yourself
in front of the people
you wanted to impress,
be yourself.
Because the universe ignores
the way that you dress,
and you have nothing to prove
to anyone.
Embrace your insignificance,
it is the purest form of freedom
any human could know.

RATCLIFFE NUNNERY

The Nuns are leaving.
They sell the cookware
and the furniture.
Call the handyman in from the orchard,
to carry out the pews.

Last year he fixed the guttering,
rabbit-proofed the vegetable patch,
fought a holy war on rats,
and landscaped the lawn.

This year he fills up boxes
with effigies from empty rooms,
sending Jesuses to Africa,
to war with Older Gods.

When he is done he pockets a crucifix
and locks the gates –
they leave nothing to remember them
in these barren rooms,
but some stained glass,
a brass plaque,
and an apple tree in bloom.

NANTGWYLLT

The dam,
as stark as stone can stand,
as raw as rock can be,
holds back the tide
that flooded out
the local history;

the houses,
gardens, gravestones,
given over to the deep.
The church bell summons
minnows here,
to join the endless sleep.

THE PEREGRINE FALCON

When I was young I held a bird
with wings larger than I,
and with a slight command
he launched into the sky,
and from above he looked at me,
with distant knowing eye,
then cawed so loud, as if to say:
What joy it is to fly.

RISE

Rise, Child,
and take your place in these stars,
they made themselves bold for your eyes.
You may not know your future, Child,
but rise.

All awaits you here,
broken into the fragments of light
that glitter so softly
in the darkened skies,
you were born,
and so may rise.

The air you breathe
was exhaled by Achilles,
so long ago
that we have fixed the flaws
that failed him.

Now you are burdened
with nothing more
than the endless possibility
of this soaring sky,
that stretches out so far
we call it infinite.

Within it you may make your home
like a God, or an eagle
that never dies.
Look to the stars,
Child, rise.

SEE THE SKY
(after J.M.W. Turner)

Have you ever seen the sky?
Seen it properly, the way the light
paints in great arcs across the sky,
the way the clouds dye themselves
into fairytale tracts of spinning light,
how the night doesn't come all at once
but in distinct stages,
    fading into a deep blue,
like the whole planet is sinking
    into the depths of the sea,
like everybody is drowning
    in the darkness together.
Like we die every night in our sleep.
Like the stars are our Gods,
    lighting paths through the deep,
like we take our time with our deaths,
and awake, reborn, with the sun.

THE RAREST OF THINGS

Human as we are
we find ourselves
building our own
private destruction,
these broken feelings
come and go, like the ocean,
the water leaves us,
but the salt remains.

But somehow
we'll always carry on,
for we are that,
the rarest of things,
beads of water
on the edge of the Earth.
Holding on,
refusing, now,
to fall.

STARDUST

I believe that
inside every heart
rests a speck of stardust,
that returns to the sky
upon our deaths.

Its weight the same
as the discrepancy found
by scientists,
weighing the dead
in search of souls.

For how else can humans
contain such wonder?
Hold such dreams?
When we are so mortal,
so small.

YOU WILL SURVIVE

If you ever feel like this world is too much,
that your mistakes are too big,
or your failures too many,
close your eyes,
breathe in this screaming air,
and speak only to yourself:
"I will survive. I will survive. I will survive."
Not for anyone else, but for yourself.
"I will survive. I will survive. I will survive."

Listen to the war drum of your heart,
spurring you on to further victories.
Listen to the wind song,
that echoes in your lungs.
Listen to the promises of trees,
the whispers of the wind,
the silent, but all pervasive
encouragement of stars.

Become one with this world in which you live
and breathe out these words once more,
make them your motto, your promise.
Scrawl them indelibly into the inside of your skull,
let them permeate every inch of your being,
make them the only thing the world
    cannot take from you:
"I will survive. I will survive. I will survive."

If you repeat something enough
    it becomes truth,
if only to those who hear it.
So speak to yourself, forever,
"I will survive. I will survive. I will survive."

You will survive.

I promise.

JAY HULME

is an award-winning poet and performer
from Leicester, winner of Slambassadors 2015 and
finalist in the 2016 Roundhouse Poetry Slam. He has
recently branched out into children's poetry and his
work was highly commended in the 2018 CLiPPA Awards.
He also works as an ambassador for Inclusive Minds,
promoting inclusion and diversity in children's
publishing while doing sensitivity reads to
ensure depictions of trans people in books
are both accurate and inoffensive.

Published by TROIKA
First published 2019

Troika Books Ltd
Well House, Green Lane, Ardleigh CO7 7PD
www.troikabooks.com

Text copyright © Jay Hulme 2019

The moral rights of the author have been asserted

A CIP catalogue record for this book is available
from the British Library

ISBN 978-1-912745-10-4

3 5 7 9 10 8 6 4

Printed in Poland at Totem.com.pl